D1389835

bran

ance

Eve
the
Knight

Level 4C

Written by Melanie Hamm
Illustrated by Bill Bolton

What is synthetic phonics?

Synthetic phonics teaches children to recognise the sounds of letters and to blend (synthesise) them together to make whole words.

Understanding sound/letter relationships gives children the confidence and ability to read unfamiliar words, without having to rely on memory or guesswork; this helps them to progress towards independent reading.

Did you know? Spoken English uses more than 40 speech sounds. Each sound is called a *phoneme*. Some phonemes relate to a single letter (d-o-g) and others to combinations of letters (sh-ar-p). When a phoneme is written down it is called a *grapheme*. Teaching these sounds, matching them to their written form and sounding out words for reading is the basis of synthetic phonics.

Consultant

I love reading phonics has been created in consultation with language expert Abigail Steel. She has a background in teaching and teacher training and is a respected expert in the field of synthetic phonics. Abigail Steel is a regular contributor to educational publications. Her international education consultancy supports parents and teachers in the promotion of literacy skills.

Reading tips

This book focuses on the ee sound, made with the letters ea, as in leaf, and the letter formation e-e as in these.

Tricky words in this book

Any words in bold may have unusual spellings or are new and have not yet been introduced.

Tricky words in this book:

were knights here thieves scheme

Extra ways to have fun with this book

After the reader has read the story, ask them questions about what they have just read:

Did you learn any new words in the book?
Which page was your favourite and why?

A round of applause for Eve the Knight!

A pronunciation guide

This grid contains the sounds used in the stories in levels 4, 5 and 6 and a guide on how to say them. /a/ represents the sounds made, rather than the letters in a word.

/ai/ as in game	/ai/ as in play/they	/ee/ as in leaf/these	/ee/ as in he
/igh/ as in kite/light	/igh/ as in find/sky	/oa/ as in home	/oa/ as in snow
/oa/ as in cold	/y+oo/ as in cube/music/new	long /oo/ as in flute/crew/blue	/oi/ as in boy
/er/ as in bird/hurt	/or/ as in snore/oar/door	/or/ as in dawn/sauce/walk	/e/ as in head
/e/ as in said/any	/ou/ as in cow	/u/ as in touch	/air/ as in hare/bear/there
/eer/ as in deer/here/cashier	/t/ as in tripped/skipped	/d/ as in rained	/j/ as in gent/gin/gym
/j/ as in barge/hedge	/s/ as in cent/circus/cyst	/s/ as in prince	/s/ as in house
/ch/ as in itch/catch	/w/ as in white	/h/ as in who	/r/ as in write/rhino

Sounds this story focuses on are highlighted in the grid.

/**f**/ as in phone	/**f**/ as in rough	/**ul**/ as in pencil/hospital	/**z**/ as in fries/cheese/breeze
/**n**/ as in knot/gnome/engine	/**m**/ as in welcome/thumb/column	/**g**/ as in guitar/ghost	/**zh**/ as in vision/beige
/**k**/ as in chord	/**k**/ as in plaque/bouquet	/**nk**/ as in uncle	/**ks**/ as in box/books/ducks/cakes
/**a**/ and /**o**/ as in hat/what	/**e**/ and /**ee**/ as in bed/he	/**i**/ and /**igh**/ as in fin/find	/**o**/ and /**oa**/ as in hot/cold
/**u**/ and short /**oo**/ as in but/put	/**ee**/, /**e**/ and /**ai**/ as in eat/bread/break	/**igh**/, /**ee**/ and /**e**/ as in tie/field/friend	/**ou**/ and /**oa**/ as in cow/blow
/**ou**/, /**oa**/ and /**oo**/ as in out/shoulder/could	/**i**/ and /**ai**/ as in money/they	/**c**/ and /**s**/ as in cat/cent	/**y**/, /**igh**/ and /**i**/ as in yes/sky/myth
/**g**/ and /**j**/ as in got/giant	/**ch**/, /**c**/ and /**sh**/ as in chin/school/chef	/**er**/, /**air**/ and /**eer**/ as in earth/bear/ears	/**u**/, /**ou**/ and /**oa**/ as in plough/dough

Be careful not to add an 'uh' sound to 's', 't', 'p', 'c', 'h', 'r', 'm', 'd', 'g', 'l', 'f' and 'b'. For example, say 'fff' not 'fuh' and 'sss' not 'suh'.

Pete and Steve **were knights**.
Eve's dream was to be a knight too.
The Queen thought about this,
and said:

"You do not look ideal, but we will test your zeal. If you can defeat the bearded beast, you will be a knight."

Eve reached the bleak mountain
peak and defeated the beast.

The King and Queen were very pleased.

"But **here** is a second feat you must complete. If you can impede three sneaky **thieves**, you will be a knight."

Eve had a clever **scheme**.
She hid herself behind a beam.

As soon as the thieves appeared to steal the gleaming gold, she impeded them.

The King and Queen were very
pleased.

"But here is a third feat you must complete. If you can feast all evening, you will be a knight."

Ten creaking tables were heaped
with treats.

Eve, Pete, Steve, and the
other knights began to eat.
They did not cease till morning.

The King and Queen were very pleased.

"But here is one final feat you must complete. If you can compete in a duel, you will be a knight."

Eve was weary but she persevered.

She competed bravely and won!

The King and Queen were very pleased. The court cheered at the joyful scene.

Said the Queen, "You may not look ideal. But we concede that you have zeal! Arise, Eve, Knight of the Four Feats!"

OVER **48** TITLES IN SIX LEVELS
Abigail Steel recommends...

Other titles to enjoy from Level 4

I love reading phonics **The Maze**
978-1-84898-559-9

I love reading phonics **Fairy Fay's Bad Day**
978-1-84898-560-5

I love reading phonics **Pirate School**
978-1-84898-566-7

Some titles from Level 5

I love reading phonics **Snapped by Sam**
978-1-84898-561-2

I love reading phonics **Max's Trip**
978-1-84898-562-9

I love reading phonics **George the Genius Gerbil**
978-1-84898-567-4

Some titles from Level 6

I love reading phonics **What Wally Wanted**
978-1-84898-563-6

I love reading phonics **Superhero Ed**
978-1-84898-564-3

I love reading phonics **The Robot Bop**
978-1-84898-570-4

An Hachette UK Company
www.hachette.co.uk

Copyright © Octopus Publishing Group Ltd 2012
First published in Great Britain in 2012 by TickTock, an imprint of Octopus Publishing Group Ltd,
Endeavour House, 189 Shaftesbury Avenue, London WC2H 8JY.
www.octopusbooks.co.uk

ISBN 978 1 84898 565 0

Printed and bound in China
10 9 8 7 6 5 4 3 2 1